Emily Eyefinger

Emily Eyefinger

Duncan Ball
Illustrated by George Ulrich

SIMON & SCHUSTER BOOKS FOR YOUNG READERS
Published by Simon & Schuster
New York   London   Toronto   Sydney   Tokyo   Singapore

SIMON & SCHUSTER BOOKS FOR YOUNG READERS
Simon & Schuster Building
Rockefeller Center
1230 Avenue of the Americas
New York, New York 10020
Text copyright © 1992 by Duncan Ball
Illustrations copyright © 1992 by George Ulrich
All rights reserved including the right of reproduction
in whole or in part in any form.
SIMON & SCHUSTER BOOKS FOR YOUNG READERS
is a trademark of Simon & Schuster.
Designed by Vicki Kalajian
Manufactured in the United States of America

10 9 8 7 6 5 4 3 2 1

Library of Congress Cataloging-in-Publication Data
Ball, Duncan   Emily Eyefinger / Duncan Ball ;
illustrated by George Ulrich.   p.   cm.
Summary: Having been born with an extra eye on the end
of her finger, Emily finds that it comes in very handy
in many unusual situations.
[1. Eye—Fiction.]
I. Ulrich, George, ill.   II. Title.   PZ7.B1985Em   1992
[Fic]—dc20   91-36345   CIP   ISBN: 0-671-74618-9

for Jill

Contents

1

Emily's Arrival

"Congratulations," the doctor said to Mrs. Eyefinger, "you have just given birth to a baby girl. A rather special baby girl," he said, hiding the baby behind his back like a present. "What are you going to name her?"

"If it were a boy we would call him Emile. But since it's a girl, she will be Emily," Mrs. Eyefinger said. She stretched her neck to see around the doctor. "What do you mean she's special? She *is* all right, isn't she?"

"Perfectly all right. It's just that little Emily's been born . . . well . . . with something extra," the doctor said. Then he held Emily out in front of him. "Have a good look."

Mrs. Eyefinger had a good look at her baby and then said, "I don't see anything extra. I just see the usual baby parts. One head, two arms, two legs. Everything seems to be in perfect order."

"Almost everything." The doctor corrected her. "Count the eyes."

"The eyes?" Mrs. Eyefinger said. "She's got two, one on either side of her nose. That's the usual number, isn't it?"

"Count again," he said, smiling from ear to ear.

Mr. and Mrs. Eyefinger looked again and saw Emily's two big blue eyes looking back.

"I'll give you a hint," the doctor said. "Look at her hands."

"At her hands?" Mr. Eyefinger said, gently uncurling his daughter's fingers.

"You see? It's on the tip of her finger," the doctor said, showing Mrs. Eyefinger. "Just like her name, Emily Eyefinger."

"Goodness me," said Mr. Eyefinger.

He held Emily's left hand and stared into the little eye on the end of his daughter's finger. There was a little eyelid on the end and it blinked once and then blinked again.

"Are many babies born like this?" Mrs. Eyefinger asked.

"Never. Well, almost never anyway," the doctor said very seriously. "I've been delivering babies for twenty years and this is the first time I've seen one."

"Why do you suppose it happened?" Mrs. Eyefinger asked.

"I'm not sure, but I have an idea," the doctor said. "Have you ever noticed that people whose last name is Slim are often thin and people named Small are often little?"

"Yes, and I suppose there are people

whose name is Little who are small," Mrs. Eyefinger added helpfully.

"And people named Cook who grow up to be cooks," Mr. Eyefinger said.

"That's different," the doctor said. "Cooks aren't cooks when they're born. They're just babies who don't know how to cook."

"They're good at eating, though," Mrs. Eyefinger said.

"If their name is Cook," Mr. Eyefinger said, "they sometimes become cooks because they can't think of what else to be."

Mr. Eyefinger nodded his head, looking proud of his explanation.

"Hmmm," said the doctor. "I'll have to think about that."

"I knew a Mrs. Sillybonnet who wore the strangest hats," Mrs. Eyefinger said.

"Did you really?" Mr. Eyefinger asked, suddenly remembering a carpenter he'd known named Ms. Hammer and a dentist named Dr. Tooth.

"Anyway, I guess life is full of surprises," the doctor said. "Your name is Eyefinger so your daughter was born with an eye on her finger. But don't worry. I see a way out of this problem."

"What problem?" asked Mr. Eyefinger.

"I can take the extra eye off," the doctor explained. "It'll be no trouble and it won't hurt little Emily at all."

"Take it off?" Mrs. Eyefinger said. "No, let's just leave it for now and see how things go. It could come in very handy," she added, chuckling at her little joke. "Very *handy*. Do you get it?"

Mr. Eyefinger and the doctor laughed a little, just to be polite.

And that was what happened the day Emily Eyefinger was born.

2

Emily's Eyefinger

Emily found that having an eye on the end of her finger could be a nuisance. You can imagine the trouble she had keeping soap out of it when she took a bath or even when she washed her hands.

And when Emily played she kept getting dust and dirt in her eyefinger. When that happened she cried and cried and cried from all three eyes at the same time. Tears ran down each cheek and a tiny tear dripped off the end of her finger.

"Poor Emily. What are we going to do?" her father asked her mother. "She keeps getting things in her eye. I never thought that having an eye on the end of your finger would be such a problem."

"I don't suppose we ever really thought about it at all," Mrs. Eyefinger said.

"I guess there are some things we don't think about until they happen," said Mr. Eyefinger. "Eyes on the ends of fingers is one of them."

"It's a good thing that the eye is on her left hand and that she's right-handed," Mrs. Eyefinger said. "If it were on her right hand, she'd be getting things in it all the time."

"If it was on her right hand, she might have turned out to be left-handed," Mr. Eyefinger said. "That's what I think anyway."

"I suppose you're right," Mrs. Eyefinger said. "Still, it does give her problems. Maybe we'd better have Emily's eye taken off."

Mr. Eyefinger sat up straight, the way people sometimes do when they get a bright idea.

"Just a minute," he said. "I have a bright idea."

With that he went to the box where he kept odds and ends. There he found a hard, round, plastic bubble from a broken compass. He took the bubble to his workbench and drilled a hole in it.

"There you go," he said, slipping it over Emily's eyefinger. "This should keep the dirt out."

"That *was* a bright idea," Mrs. Eyefinger said. "We can put some tape on it so it won't fall off. Then Emily can play and even wash herself without hurting her eye."

Everything was a little blurry when Emily looked through the plastic bubble with her eyefinger. Now and then a little bit of soapy water or dirt did get into the bubble and into

Emily's eye. But most of the time it worked perfectly.

When Grandmother Eyefinger came to visit, Emily held out her finger to show her the plastic bubble.

"Dada," Emily said.

"No, *finger*," said Grandmother Eyefinger. "Can you say *finger?*"

Emily shook her head and frowned.

"*Dada*," she said again.

"She means that her father made that bubble cover for her eye," Mrs. Eyefinger explained.

"Oh, Dada made that," her grandmother said. Emily smiled from ear to ear. " Wasn't that clever of Dada?"

Emily knew she was lucky to have a father who was full of bright ideas.

When Emily learned to walk, her parents let her play outside. There was a big fence that went all around the yard to keep her from going into the street.

One day Mrs. Eyefinger came home from shopping. She parked in front of the house. As soon as she got out of the car she heard Emily's voice saying, "Mommy. Mommy. I see Mommy."

Mrs. Eyefinger stopped and looked at the fence but there was no sign of Emily.

"I see Mommy. Mommy don't see me," Emily said again.

"Mommy *doesn't* see me." Her mother corrected her. "Where are you? I can hear you but I can't see you."

"Here, Mommy, here," Emily said and then she giggled.

Mrs. Eyefinger looked down and saw a little finger poking under the bottom of the fence. It was Emily's eyefinger!

"Where oh where can Emily be?" Mrs. Eyefinger said. "Where oh where can she be?"

11

Mrs. Eyefinger threw open the gate and snatched Emily up in her arms.

"Gotcha!" she said. "You little rascal! You were spying on me!"

"Silly Mommy," said Emily and she laughed long and loud.

It was the first time she had fooled her mother. And it was a lot of fun.

One Sunday all of Emily's relatives came to dinner. There were big Eyefingers and small Eyefingers and old Eyefingers and young Eyefingers. There were even some relatives who weren't Eyefingers at all. Of course none of them had eyes on their fingers except Emily.

Grandfather Eyefinger did some magic tricks. First he made a golf ball disappear. And then he made it come out of Emily's ear. Then three golf balls came out of his mouth and he found another one in Emily's pocket.

She didn't even know it was there until he found it. Emily loved his magic tricks. Grandfather was a very special man.

Later, Emily's cousin Sally came up behind her and put her hands over her face.

"Guess who?" said Sally.

Emily just pointed her eyefinger over her shoulder to see who it was.

"It's Sally," she said.

Sally laughed. They all wished they had eyes on their fingers.

When they were sitting at the table eating cherry cobbler, Emily suddenly climbed down from her high chair. She went around the table, looking at everyone's hands. Her grandfather's fingers were hidden in big stiff fists. Emily had to uncurl them one by one to see their ends.

"What are you doing, Emily?" he asked in a wobbly voice. "The golf balls are all gone."

"She's looking for your eyefinger," Mrs.

Eyefinger said with a wink. "She does it all the time now. She's looking to see if anyone else has an eyefinger. She even does it when we go to the supermarket."

Some of her cousins giggled and then everyone laughed. Emily let go of her grandfather's hands and began to cry.

"Oh, Emily," Grandfather Eyefinger said, hugging her. "Don't cry. No one's laughing at you."

"I don't want my eyefinger," Emily said. "Take it away."

Then her cousin Wilbur said, "If you don't want it, can I have it?"

And her cousin Sally said, "No, I want it!"

And her cousin Betsy said, "I want it too! I've always wanted to have an eyefinger."

Sally picked Emily up and put her over her shoulder. Then she ran to the other side of the dining table.

"It's mine!" Sally yelled. "It's mine! I get to have an eyefinger!"

14

Wilbur and Betsy chased Sally and Emily around and around the table, yelling and screaming.

"Stay away from us!" Sally yelled.

Emily's stomach was beginning to hurt from all the jiggling. Sally threw her down on the couch. They all three started pulling at her eyefinger (but not very hard).

"It's mine! It's mine!" Wilbur yelled. "Emily doesn't want it so it's mine."

"Look!" Betsy said. They all stopped pulling. "It's stuck on. How are we ever going to get it off? I think Emily is just going to have to keep it."

Emily was still crying but she smiled. They all wanted an eyefinger. But she was the only one in the world who could have one. She knew she was very special — just like Grandfather.

3

Emily at Home

Emily grew bigger and bigger and so did her eyefinger. Her father had to keep making the hole in the bubble bigger so it wouldn't be too tight. Sometimes Emily hurt her eyefinger and wished she didn't have it. But at other times it was very useful, like the time when Mrs. Eyefinger lost her earring.

"I've looked everywhere for it," her mother said. "But there are some places I can't see, like under the piano and under the car seats."

Emily poked her eyefinger under the piano. There was nothing there but dust.

Then she got into the car and put her eyefinger under the seats. She found a couple of coins but no earring.

"I know," Mrs. Eyefinger said. "Let's look down behind the stove, shall we? Things have a way of losing themselves behind stoves. I don't know why but they do."

Emily pointed her eyefinger down behind the stove.

"I spy with my little eye something you wear on your ear," she said.

"You're an angel," her mother said. Mrs. Eyefinger put a piece of chewing gum on the end of a broom handle. "I'll poke this down there and you tell me where the earring is."

Emily told her to move it a little this way and then a little that way.

"You're right over it now," Emily said.

Her mother stabbed the broom handle down. Then she pulled it up. Sure enough, there was the earring stuck in the chewing gum.

"Icky-poo," Mrs. Eyefinger said, pulling the earring out of the gum. "How will I ever get all this guck off it? It's all your fault for having that eye on your finger."

Emily frowned. Then she grabbed the earring out of her mother's hand and dangled it behind the stove.

"Emily! What are you doing?" Mrs. Eyefinger asked.

"I'm going to drop it," Emily said.

"Sweetheart, I was only kidding about your eyefinger!" Mrs. Eyefinger said.

"So was I," Emily said, and they both laughed. "How would you like some other things?" Emily asked.

"What things?"

"A spoon, two forks, a potholder, a clothes pin, and a tennis ball."

"Down there? Behind the stove?"

Emily nodded.

"That's what I mean about things losing

themselves behind stoves. You're a very use-ful little girl," Mrs. Eyefinger said. "I don't know what I'd do without your eyefinger. I promise never to make jokes about it again."

And she never did.

When Mr. and Mrs. Eyefinger went to the movies, they often asked Carol Singer (who was a very good singer) to babysit. Carol lived down the street. She was in high school. Before she started babysitting, Mrs. Eyefinger went over to Carol's house to talk to her.

"Emily isn't exactly like other little girls," Mrs. Eyefinger began.

"No one is exactly the same," Carol said.

"That's true," said Mrs. Eyefinger.

"People are all different," Carol went on. "Sort of like snowflakes. We're all different."

"Yes, Carol, I know. But Emily is really *quite* a different little snowflake."

"What do you mean, Mrs. Eyefinger?"

"There is something special about her that I think you should know."

"I'm sure there is," Carol said. She wondered what Mrs. Eyefinger was trying to say.

Mrs. Eyefinger thought for a minute. Finally she held up her hands.

"Look at these," she said.

"Yes?"

"What do you see?"

"Fingers?" asked Carol.

"And what is on the end of each of them?"

Maybe Mrs. Eyefinger liked guessing games, Carol thought.

"Oh, I know. Fingernails!" said Carol.

"Exactly," Mrs. Eyefinger said. "I have a fingernail on each and every one of my fingers."

Carol looked at her own fingers. She had fingernails on all of hers too.

"Oh, I get it," Carol said with a laugh. "You're trying to tell me about the eye on

20

the end of Emily's finger, aren't you, Mrs. Eyefinger?"

"So you know about it."

"Mom told me. She's a doctor in the hospital. She knew about Emily's finger the day she was born."

"And it doesn't bother you?" Mrs. Eyefinger asked carefully.

"Bother me? Heavens no. I think it's great," Carol said. "I wish I had an eye on the end of *my* finger. It would be very useful for finding things. Have you ever noticed how things are always losing themselves behind stoves?"

"I certainly have," said Mrs. Eyefinger.

When Carol Singer looked after Emily, she sang songs to her. (Sometimes she even sang carols.) She always read books to her, especially books about animals. Emily wanted to know everything there was to know about animals. She loved it when Carol came to babysit.

One day Carol taught Emily how to play Hide and Seek.

"Put your hands over your face," she told Emily, "and count to ten. I'll go away and hide. Then you say, 'Here I come, ready or not,' and see if you can find me. Get it?"

Emily looked puzzled.

"Come on, Emily. It's easy."

Emily put her hands over her face and began to count to ten. She watched with her eyefinger as Carol got down on her hands and knees and crawled behind the couch. When she finished counting, Emily said, "Here I come, ready or not," just the way Carol had said. Then Emily crawled right behind the couch and bumped straight into Carol's bottom.

"Hey," Carol said. "How did you find me so fast?"

"I saw you," Emily said. "I did what you told me to do."

Now Carol was puzzled.

"You saw me?" Carol said. "But you were supposed to put your hands over your face."

"I did," said Emily.

Emily put her hands over her face and Carol saw her eyefinger. She gave a big laugh.

"I completely forgot about your extra eye," Carol said. "You have to keep it closed too, or it's cheating. No wonder you didn't understand the game."

Carol gave Emily a big hug.

"Come on now," Carol said. "Let's play it the right way."

After that Emily and Carol played lots of games of Hide and Seek. Emily always kept the eyelid on her finger closed when she was counting.

Emily loved playing Hide and Seek with Carol. She could peek around corners and into closets with her eyefinger. When she saw Carol she would say, "I spy with my little eye someone who starts with C."

When Emily was hiding she could watch with her eyefinger and see Carol coming. Then it wasn't so scary when Carol found her.

4

Emily Gets a Pet

One evening just before her birthday Emily and her parents were playing Go Fish. Emily did not feel very well that day. She had taken the bubble cover off her eye and had fallen down and bumped it. The eye was all red and sore.

Mrs. Eyefinger asked Emily if she wanted the doctor to take the eye off.

"Then you wouldn't have to bother with finger bubbles," she said. "You'd be just like everyone else."

"I don't want to be just like everyone else,"

Emily said, dealing out the cards with her eyefinger closed so she wouldn't see them. "At least not yet. I love my eyefinger even if it bothers me sometimes. I can do things that nobody else can. I'm so lucky to have it."

"I guess eyefingers don't grow on trees," her father said.

"What does that mean?"

"When someone says that something doesn't grow on trees, it means that there aren't many of them around. Eyes on the end of fingers certainly don't grow on trees."

"That's true," Emily said.

"Hmmm," said her father as he looked at his cards.

"Give me all your aces," Emily said.

Mr. Eyefinger wanted to say, "Fish," but instead he started to pick out his aces to give to Emily. "Are you sure that you didn't peek at my cards with that eyefinger of yours?" he asked.

Mr. Eyefinger smiled. He only said it to be funny. He knew that Emily would never ever cheat.

"Don't be a bad sport, Dad," Emily said. "You know I would never ever cheat. I'm just lucky."

"That's true," he said, handing over three aces.

"Okay, Mom. Give me all your fives," Emily said.

Mrs. Eyefinger looked through her cards. She picked out two fives and gave them to Emily.

"By the way," Emily's mother said. "What do you want for your birthday?"

Emily thought for a minute.

"Fish," she said.

"Just a minute," her mother said. "It's still your turn. I'm the one who's supposed to say 'Fish'."

"No. Not that kind of fish," said Emily. "I

want a fish for my birthday. A pet fish in a fish bowl."

"Oh, a *real* fish," said Mrs. Eyefinger. "We'll see what we can do."

Emily's first pet was the fish she got for her birthday. It was a goldfish in a nice round bowl. Emily watched it swim around and around and around the bowl.

"Do you think he's happy?" she asked.

"Of course he's happy," her father said. "He lives in a nice house and has a nice little girl to feed him. What more could a goldfish want?"

"I suppose you're right," Emily said. "He does look happy."

"That's the important thing," her father said. "A goldfish that looks happy is a happy goldfish. That's what I always say."

When her mother asked her what she was going to name him, Emily said, "I think I'll call him Fluffy."

"Fluffy?" Mrs. Eyefinger said. "You can't name a goldfish Fluffy."

"Why not?" asked Emily.

"Because he's not fluffy. Kittens are fluffy. Fish are slippery. Why don't you call him Slippery or Slick or Slimy?"

"I don't like Slippery or Slick or Slimy. He *is* fluffy," Emily insisted.

Mrs. Eyefinger put on her glasses and looked at the little fish swimming around.

"Explain to me what is fluffy about this fish," she said.

"His tail," Emily said.

Mrs. Eyefinger looked again at the goldfish's wide tail.

"The tail is lacy," Emily's mother said. "It's not fluffy, it's *lacy*. I know! You could call him Lacy."

"Lacy sounds too much like Lucy," Emily said. "And Lucy just isn't a good fish name. I still like Fluffy best."

The next day, Emily's mother came home

with a book and gave it to Emily. It was called *Naming Your Goldfish*. Emily and her mother looked at the book. There were lots of pretty pictures of goldfish in it.

"Is he a boy or a girl?" Mrs. Eyefinger said. "That's the first question."

Mr. Eyefinger looked up from his newspaper.

"He's a boy," he said.

"How can you tell?" Mrs. Eyefinger asked.

"He's are always boys. She's are always girls. You said, 'Is *he* a boy or a girl'."

"Very funny," Mrs. Eyefinger said. "But is *it* a boy or is *it* a girl?"

"Now that's a different question," Mr. Eyefinger said. "I don't have any idea."

"What do you think, Emily?"

Emily shrugged. She wished that no one had said anything about names.

"I'll read you some names," Mrs. Eyefinger said. "You can pick the right one. How about Aaron?"

"No," Emily said.

"Abigail?"

"No."

"Abelard?"

"No."

"Adriana?"

"No."

Mrs. Eyefinger read through hundreds and hundreds of names. There were names like Mirabel and Montague and Sharleen and Skipper and even names like Trinette and Theobald and Wulstan and Walburga.

"He doesn't look like a Walburga to me," Mrs. Eyefinger said. "Does he to you?"

Emily just shook her head. Mrs. Eyefinger closed the book and threw it on the couch.

"Not a very useful book," she said. "I'm sorry I bought it."

Emily sprinkled some fish food on top of the water. The goldfish came up to eat it. His mouth was shaped like a perfect O. He ate the bits of food and then went back down.

"I've made up my mind," Emily announced. "I've decided that he's a boy and I'm going to call him Fluffy. I don't care if it's a good name or a bad name. I don't even care if it's the *right* name."

Emily had made up her mind and that was that.

Then she put the bubble on her eyefinger and put it down in the water. She looked Fluffy straight in the eye. He wasn't frightened. He looked as though he'd seen hundreds of eyefingers. And he never looked happier.

One morning Emily got up and couldn't find Fluffy. He wasn't in his bowl.

"Mom!" she cried. "Fluffy's escaped!"

"Don't panic, dear," her mother said. "He probably just jumped out of the bowl. Goldfish do that sometimes by accident. Let's look around on the floor and see if we can find him."

Emily and her mother got down on their hands and knees and looked. But there was no sign of Fluffy.

"I know!" Emily said. "Maybe he's under the bookcase."

Emily wiggled her eyefinger under the bottom of the bookcase. Sure enough, there was Fluffy. Emily reached in and picked him up. He was all covered with dust. She very carefully put him back in his bowl. The little fish lay on his side at the bottom. Then he straightened up and started swimming slowly around the bowl. All the dust fell away and he looked like his old self again.

"Is he going to be all right?" Emily asked.

"Yes, darling. I think you found him just in time," her mother said. "Fish can't live out of water for very long. You're so lucky that you have an eye on your finger."

"It's lucky for me and it's lucky for Fluffy," said Emily.

"And you chose just the right name," Mrs.

Eyefinger said. "All that dust made him look very fluffy."

Emily put *Naming Your Goldfish* on top of the bowl, leaving a tiny space at the side for air. Now Fluffy couldn't jump out again.

"You see?" she said. "It's a very useful book."

And they both laughed.

5

Emily Goes to School

Emily had a cold on the first day of school so she didn't go until the next day. On the first day, when Emily was still sick, her new teacher, Ms. Plump (who was just a little overweight), gave the class a special talk. She said that they should all be nice to Emily when she came the next day.

"Don't look at the eye on the end of her finger," Ms. Plump said. "It might embarrass her. Just pretend you don't notice it."

The next day Emily's mother brought her to school and all the children sat silently at their desks looking a little scared.

"Class, I'd like you to say 'good morning' to our new student, Emily Eyefinger," Ms. Plump said.

"Good morning, Emily Eyefinger," the children said very slowly, the way children do when they're asked to say 'good morning' all together. They looked in every direction, trying not to look at Emily's finger.

Then Simon Sickly, who had also been sick the day before and had missed Ms. Plump's little talk, yelled, "Hey look! Her name's Eyefinger and she's got an eye on the end of her finger!"

Before Ms. Plump could scold him, Emily laughed a big laugh. Then the whole class laughed and even Ms. Plump laughed along with them.

"Yes, I do have an eye on the end of my finger," Emily said, holding it up for everyone to see. "Here, take a good look."

That day Emily made twenty-five good friends all at once.

A month later, a new boy started school. His name was Terry Meaney and he was a real bully. He wore dirty white socks that smelled terrible and he never smiled.

Now the thing about bullies is this: they look for anyone who is different and then start picking on them. They only pick on children who are smaller than they are. But Terry was very big for his age so he could pick on anyone he wanted to.

For the first few days Terry just sat quietly in class looking grumpy. Then one day at recess he saw Emily's eyefinger.

"Hey, you," he said, "what's that thing on your finger?"

"It's an eye," Emily explained.

"Does it work?"

"Of course it does."

Emily took off the bubble. She looked at him through her eyefinger and he looked back.

"That's stupid," Terry said. "That's the stupidest thing I ever seen."

"You mean it's the stupidest thing you *have* ever seen."

"Ha ha ha ha ha," Terry sang. "She's got an eye on her finger. She's got an eye on her finger. Ha ha ha ha ha. That's really stupid. Ha ha ha ha ha."

The other children stopped playing. They were all afraid of Terry Meaney. They thought he was going to beat Emily up.

"Ha ha ha ha ha," Terry sang again, pointing to Emily.

Emily was patient at first. Then she said, "I'm sorry, Terry, but you can't have one. They don't grow on trees, you know."

"What do you mean?" Terry asked.

"You want an eye on the end of your finger, but you can't have one," Emily said. "They don't grow on trees, you know."

Terry wasn't expecting her to say this. He was completely baffled.

"Oh yes I can have one," he said angrily.

"Oh no you can't. You have to be born with one," Emily explained. "That's the only way to get an eyefinger. You weren't born with one so that's too bad for you. Too late. Bad luck."

"My dad said he can get me one," Terry said. "He says I can have anything I want."

"You may be able to have lots of things but you definitely can't have an eyefinger."

"Yes I CAN."

"No you can't."

"Yes I CAN."

"You do want one, don't you?" Emily said.

Terry had to think for a minute. He knew Emily had tricked him, but he didn't know what to say.

"I could have one if I wanted," Terry said.

"But I don't want one because it looks stupid."

Just then the bell rang and the children started back into the school. Emily smiled and wiggled her eyefinger at Terry. Then she put the bubble over it again and put her hand in her pocket.

"I'll get you," Terry said. (Bullies always say, "I'll get you.")

"No you won't," Emily said back. "And you won't get an eyefinger either."

Every time Terry tried to pick on Emily, she made him feel silly. So he stopped picking on her. But he kept right on picking on the other children.

Terry sat in class looking grumpy. He gave everybody angry looks.

"That Terry Meaney is a real meany," Emily thought. "I'll have to come up with a plan to stop him from being a bully. Hmmm. I don't know how, but *I'm going to get him!*"

6

Emily Ghost Finger

Emily's chance to get Terry came one day when all the children were talking about ghosts. Janey Star said that her aunt knew someone who had seen a ghost. Then Annabelle said that her uncle had seen a ghost too. Then Emma said that her mother had seen a ghost when she went to her grandmother's farm. Jonathan's brother had seen a ghost when he spent the night at a friend's house. Everybody had something to say about ghosts.

By the time lunchtime was over Emily's

whole class was scared of ghosts. But Terry was bragging. He said he'd seen lots and lots of ghosts, maybe even a hundred of them. He said he saw them all the time.

"They don't scare me," he said. "I laugh at ghosts. Ha ha ha!"

Emily didn't believe in ghosts. But suddenly she had an idea.

"You'd better not say that, Terry," she said.

"I can say whatever I want," he said.

Emily's eyes narrowed. "If you do," she whispered, "they'll come and get you."

"I'm not scared of any stupid ghost," Terry said. "If one ever did anything to me I'd get him back."

"That's what you think," said Emily.

"That's what I know," said Terry.

When the class started again, the children were sitting quietly in their chairs.

"My my," Ms. Plump said. "Such long faces. Is anything wrong?"

"Annabelle's uncle saw a ghost," Janey said.

"And so did Jonathan's brother," Annabelle said.

Ms. Plump laughed.

"You're a bunch of silly billies," she said. "There aren't any such things as ghosts. They're all in your heads. You've just frightened yourselves. Now sit up straight. We're going to have a spelling lesson."

On the way home from school, Terry was still on the lookout for ghosts. He looked all around as he walked. He kept looking over his shoulder to make sure nothing was following him.

He turned the corner and a slow deep voice said, "Terry Meaney, I see you."

Terry stopped and looked around. But no one was there, only a big blue mailbox. He started shaking all over.

"Who said that?" he said.

"I did," the voice said. "You can't see me because I'm a ghost."

Terry smiled a nervous smile.

The voice said, "What are you smiling at? This isn't funny."

"Wh-Wh-Where are you?"

Terry couldn't think of anything else to say. He was scared silly.

"I'm right in front of you. I can see you but you can't see me. I'm invisible. Are you laughing at me?"

"N-N-No," said Terry.

"I hear that you laugh at ghosts."

"I don't! It's not true!"

"You said that you did. I heard you say it."

"I was kidding. I never laughed at a ghost! Please don't hurt me," Terry pleaded. "Please!"

"Say 'pretty please.'"

"Pretty please. Pretty please. Pretty please," Terry said. His knees were knocking together so much that he could hardly stand up. "I'll do anything you say!"

"Change those smelly socks! They're horrible!"

Terry looked down at his dirty socks.

"Another thing . . ." the voice said.

Terry had turned as white as a sheet. His mouth opened in the shape of a perfect O, just like Fluffy's. He turned around in a circle, looking for the ghost. He didn't see Emily's eyefinger poking over the top of the mailbox.

"Wh-Wh-What is it?" Terry stammered.

Emily said in her deepest voice: "Stop picking on people."

"I don't pick on people. Honest, I don't."

"Don't lie to me, Terry Meaney! Ghosts know everything! If you ever pick on anybody again, I'm going to get you!"

"I won't! I promise I won't!" Terry cried. "Please don't get me!"

"Okay, you can go now," Emily said. "I'm tired of looking at you."

Terry ran away as fast as he could.

And from then on the children noticed a big change in Terry. He didn't pick on anybody. He didn't tell Emily that her eyefinger was stupid. Sometimes he even smiled and talked to the other children. He was a nice boy, really. And his socks were always remarkably clean.

7

Emily at the Zoo

Most of the time Emily's life was just like anyone else's. But she had to remember certain things, like being careful not to hit her finger. And to take the bubble cover with her when she went out. Sometimes she put her hand in her pocket so people wouldn't stare or ask her about her eyefinger. But mostly she didn't care what people thought.

One day Mrs. Eyefinger took Emily and her friend Janey Star to the zoo. (Janey wanted to be a movie star.) Mrs. Star came along too.

Emily had been there many times before.

She loved animals. She wanted to learn everything about them that she could. Janey had never been to any zoo. The only place she'd seen wild animals was on television. She didn't really want to go. It was Emily's idea.

Emily walked through the zoo telling Janey lots of things about animals. Mrs. Eyefinger and Mrs. Star walked behind.

"Did you know that elephants keep growing as long as they live?" Emily asked Janey.

"No, I didn't."

"It's true," Emily said. "And did you know that the ostrich is the biggest bird in the world?"

"No, I didn't."

"And that all insects have six legs?"

"Really?"

"Spiders have eight legs. They're not insects," Emily added.

"They're still bugs," Janey said. "I don't like bugs."

51

"And did you know that giraffes have seven bones in their necks just like people?"

"Is that true?" Janey asked politely.

"Cross my heart," Emily said. "I read it in a book. Did you know that owls can turn their heads backward without moving the rest of them? Their eyes can't move so they have to turn their heads."

"Very interesting," Janey said. But she really wasn't interested.

"I can see behind myself too," Emily laughed, pointing her finger behind her. She looked at her mother and Janey's mother. "And did you know that—"

"Stop!" Janey said. "I can't remember all those things."

"Do you want me to tell them to you again?" Emily asked.

"No. It's too much. You be the animal expert. I don't care about animals. I just want to be a movie star."

Emily couldn't imagine why anyone would want to be a movie star.

Mrs. Eyefinger and Mrs. Star were busy talking.

"You two go on ahead," Mrs. Star called out. "We'll catch up with you."

Emily led Janey to the snake house. The snakes were all in glass cages.

"Snakes give me the creeps," Janey said. "They make me shiver just to look at them."

"Snakes can open their mouths really wide. They can eat things that are bigger than their heads," Emily said. "Some of them wrap themselves around small animals and squeeze them to fit them into their mouths."

"That's disgusting," Janey said. "Snakes are horrible!"

"It's nature," said Emily. "That's just the way they are. They can't help it."

"I still don't like them," Janey said. "Let's get out of here!"

Just then a keeper appeared.

"She's gone! She's gone!" he yelled. "The anaconda isn't in her cage!"

Sure enough, the glass in one cage was broken. Emily looked in. There was no snake inside. Emily knew that an anaconda was a very big snake of the squeezing kind.

Soon other keepers came running. The people who had been looking at the snakes hurried away. They decided that they would rather be somewhere else. Somewhere where there weren't any missing snakes.

Keepers dashed around peering into cracks and down holes. They even looked up in the trees for the lost snake. But they couldn't find her anywhere.

Emily was having fun watching all the excitement. Janey wasn't. She was so frightened that she couldn't even move. She just stood there, trembling.

One of the keepers noticed Janey.

"I'm the head keeper," she said. "Is there

something wrong with you? Are you sick or something?"

"She doesn't like snakes very much," Emily said. "I think she's frightened."

"Don't worry," the head keeper said to Janey. "Anna is a harmless old snake. She doesn't bite people. She can't even squeeze her food anymore. She only eats pre-squozen food. There's absolutely nothing to worry about."

Then she hurried off.

"Did you hear that?" Emily asked. "Anna is harmless."

Janey stopped shivering.

"All right, but let's go," she said.

Just as they were leaving, Emily saw something strange. There was a long pipe, one of those drains that takes rainwater down from the roof. As she looked at it, it wiggled a tiny bit.

"I think that pipe just wiggled," Emily said. "I wonder if Anna is in there."

"If she is," Janey said, "I'm sure the keepers will find her."

"They can't," Emily said. "The pipe is all bendy at the bottom and at the top. They can't possibly see in it. They can't see around corners."

"Can we just go?" Janey asked.

Emily got down on her knees and put her hand into the drainpipe. It was a big pipe and her hand fit in easily. She poked her finger around the bend. Then she opened the eyelid on her eyefinger and peered up into the darkness. Sure enough, there was Anna Anaconda's tail way up in the pipe.

"I've found her!" she called out. "Anna's in here!"

The keepers stopped what they were doing. They hurried over to Emily.

"Can we just go?" Janey whispered to Emily.

"How do you know she's in there?" the head keeper asked. "Are you touching her?"

"No, I'm looking at her," Emily said.

The keepers were all very puzzled. Some of them started scratching their heads.

Emily pulled her hand out of the drain pipe and pulled the bubble off the end of her finger. She held it up proudly for everyone to see.

"Goodness!" a keeper said. "I've never seen one of those."

"No," said Emily. "Most people haven't. I think I have the only one."

"Well, I'll be a monkey's uncle," the head keeper said. "An eye on the end of her finger. What's it like having an eye on the end of your finger?"

"It's good but it does cause some problems," Emily said. "So on the one hand, I like it. But on the other hand, I don't."

Everyone laughed and Emily realized she'd made a joke.

In a few minutes the keepers had taken down the drain pipe. The big snake slid out onto the ground. Two of the keepers picked Anna up and she gave them a little hug as they put her in a big wooden box.

"Just for helping us," the head keeper said, "you girls can come to the zoo any time you want. It won't cost you anything."

Emily was overjoyed.

"Thank you very much," she said.

"You're very welcome," the head keeper said. "If we ever lose a snake again, we'll know just who to call."

"Can we go *now*?" Janey asked.

"Not until we take a picture for the newspaper," the head keeper said, pulling out a camera. "Now hold that finger eye thing up so we can all see it."

And that was how Emily and Janey got their picture on the front page of the newspaper.

"Now we're famous," Janey told Emily. "I like being famous. Thanks for taking me to the zoo, Emily."

8

Emily's Adventure at Sea

One day Emily's class took a trip to an island in a boat. After eating dozens of sandwiches and four whole chocolate-fudge layercakes, the children climbed back on the boat. But before they got home a blanket of fog rolled in. No one could see a thing.

"This is terrible," Captain Sailwell (who was a very good sailor) said as he dropped anchor and stopped the boat. "I don't know how we're going to get home. Here we are out in the water with rocks all around us. If we run into a rock, the boat will surely sink.

I've never been in such thick fog. Why, I can't even see the nose in front of my face."

"I can see the nose in front of my face," Emily said, pointing her finger at her nose. "But I don't know what good that will do."

The captain thought for a moment. Then he snapped his fingers. His eyes opened wide and his jaw dropped.

"Did you just get a bright idea?" Ms. Plump asked.

"No, I just remembered that I left my foghorn on the kitchen table this morning," the captain said. "Oh, what a terrible mess! What am I going to do?"

"*I* have a bright idea," Ms. Plump said, trying to snap her fingers but not making any noise. "Emily can stretch out her arm and use her eyefinger to look for rocks. She has an eye on the end of her finger, you know."

"An eye on the end of her finger?" Captain Sailwell said. "What will they think of next?

Wait! Didn't I see you in the newspaper?"

"Yes," Emily said with a smile.

"Well, that eye thing certainly must be *handy*," he said with a giggle.

"Would you mind looking for rocks, Emily?" Ms. Plump asked.

"I'd be happy to," Emily said.

Emily stood in the bow and pointed her finger into the fog.

"Can you see any anything?" Captain Sailwell asked. "I think there are some rocks right in front of us."

"I can't see anything," said Emily. She took off the bubble to see more clearly. "The fog is too thick. I can't see far enough ahead."

"You are looking through that—that finger of yours, aren't you?" the captain asked.

"Yes, of course," answered Emily.

"If only your arm were longer," Captain Sailwell said. "I suppose it will be longer a few years from now. But we can't wait that long, can we?"

"I know!" Emily said. (It was her turn for a bright idea.) "Why don't I go out on the pointy stick?"

"What pointy stick? For heaven's sake, girl," said Captain Sailwell. "What are you talking about? There aren't any pointy sticks on boats. Everything has a proper name. There are masts and there are booms but no pointy sticks. Now what are you talking about?"

"That thing on the front of the boat," Emily said, pointing to what she meant.

"Oh, *that* pointy stick," Captain Sailwell mumbled. "I never did know the name of that thing. What about it?"

"If I climb up on that, my finger will be way out front. Then I could see farther ahead."

"Well, I'll be dipped," Captain Sailwell said. "Now there's a bright idea."

Captain Sailwell and Ms. Plump tied a safety line to Emily in case she fell off. Then

they lifted her up and helped her out on the pointy stick at the front of the boat.

"Okay," Emily said. "You can pull up the anchor. But go very slowly, please."

And so it was that Emily saved her entire class. She called out, "Rock on the right!" and "Rock on the left!" and "Rock straight ahead" until the captain had steered the boat safely back to shore.

Captain Sailwell hauled her in and Emily went ashore. Everyone was very happy, even Terry Meaney.

"You can come sailing with me anytime," the captain told Emily. "Especially when it's foggy."

9

Emily's Mouse

One morning in May, Emily and her parents drove to a place in the country where people used to dig for gold. All over a grassy hill they saw hundreds of deep holes that had once been mines.

"It's a good place to have a rest and be out in nature. But we'll have to be very careful and not fall in a hole," Emily's mother said. "Please don't skip, Emily. It makes me nervous."

Emily didn't skip. She was extremely careful as she walked around. She stopped now and then and poked her finger into the grass.

"What are you looking for, dear?" Mr. Eyefinger asked.

"Insects," said Emily.

"Insects?" her father asked her. "Creepy crawleys?"

"You know I love animals," Emily said.

"Yes, I know," said Mr. Eyefinger.

When Emily wanted to look down in a mine, she lay on the ground and crawled up to it, peeping carefully over the edge with her finger.

Later, while Emily and her parents were lying on a blanket, a head popped up out of one of the holes.

"Help!" it screamed.

"Help?" asked Mr. Eyefinger, who couldn't think of anything else to say.

"Yes, help!" the man said again, and he scrambled up a rope and out of the hole. "My son is down there. He can't get out."

"We'll go for help," Mr. Eyefinger said.

"There's no time," the man answered. "He could suffocate. You see, he wriggled down a very narrow tunnel and now he's stuck. I tried to get a rope around his foot so I could pull him loose, but the tunnel is too small and I can't get close enough to him."

"What were you doing down there?" Mr. Eyefinger asked.

"My name is Professor Mousefinder and I look for certain . . . er . . . small furry animals that live down holes."

"Mice?" asked Emily. "Is that what you look for?"

"Why, yes. How did you know?"

"I just guessed," Emily said.

"My son, Malcolm, and I were looking for a rare kind of mouse. Malcolm saw one and followed it into the tunnel. Please, does anyone have any idea of how to rescue him?"

"I'm the smallest one here," Emily said. "I will try to rescue your son."

"I'm afraid you're not as small as my Malcolm," the professor said. "Besides, he's squiggled around a very narrow corner. You'd have to be able to see around corners even to find him."

"I *can* see around corners," Emily said, showing him her eyefinger.

"Good grief!" the professor cried. "You've got an eye on the end of your finger. Yuck! Oh, I am sorry I said that," he added.

"That's all right," Emily said. "Don't be embarrassed. Lots of people are surprised to see an eye on the end of a finger."

And so it was that they gave Emily a flashlight and lowered her down to the bottom of the hole. She quickly found the tiny tunnel and crawled along until she couldn't go any farther.

"Are you in there, Malcolm?"

There was a muffled noise up ahead that sounded like, "Uuummmppphhhh, ooooorr-rrrmmmmmpppppph!"

"Everything's all right," Emily said. "I'm Emily Eyefinger and I've come to rescue you."

"Uuuuoooooooppppprrrmmmmmpppphh!"

Emily put the flashlight in her eyefinger hand and reached around a very narrow corner. With her eyefinger she could see the bottoms of Malcolm's shoes. She quickly untied the rope from her waist and reached around the corner to tie his feet. But they were too far away.

Emily pulled the rope back and made a loop at the end. Then she reached around again and threw the loop toward Malcolm. Time after time she threw it but missed his feet. Finally she caught them. She pulled the rope tight around them.

"Thank goodness I have my eyefinger," she said to herself. "If I didn't, I wouldn't have been able to do this."

"Uuuuoooooooppppprrrmmmmmpppphh!"

Malcolm cried again, this time much louder than the time before.

Then Emily squirmed back out of the tunnel and stood at the bottom of the hole.

"Hello up there," she called.

Suddenly three heads peered down at her.

"Did you find him?" asked Professor Mousefinder. "Is he all right?"

"He's fine," Emily said. "I tied the rope around his feet. Now all you have to do is pull."

"Okay, everybody pull!" Mrs. Eyefinger cried.

The rope grew tight and then began shooting past Emily. She stepped back against the dirt wall as the rope went faster and faster. Dust and dirt filled the air, and Emily quickly put her eyefinger hand in her pocket. Down the tunnel Emily heard a long scream that got louder and louder.

"YiiiiiiooooooOOWWWWWWW!"

Finally a big dirty lump shot from the end of the tunnel and dangled upside down in the hole. The lump was Malcolm, and he was screaming louder than ever.

"HEEEEEELP!" he cried.

In his hands he clutched a small mouse.

"You're safe now!" Emily said.

"HEEEEEELP!" Malcolm cried again.

The rope jerked and he went flying up.

After a minute or two, Emily's parents and the two Mousefinders peeked down the hole again.

"Are you okay down there?" Professor Mousefinder asked.

"I'm fine," said Emily. "But I wouldn't mind if you pulled me up."

"Yes, of course," said Professor Mousefinder.

He threw down the rope and they all pulled Emily to safety.

"Thank you very much, Emily. If it hadn't

been for that eye thing on your finger," Professor Mousefinder said, "I'm sure I would have lost little Malcolm."

"And we never would have discovered this," Malcolm said, patting the mouse. "I've never seen one like it."

"No one has," said the professor. "Today we've discovered a new kind of mouse. Can you think of a name for it?"

"I know," said Malcolm. "Let's name it after Emily."

"What a good idea," said Professor Mousefinder. "We'll call it *Mus emiliensis*. That's the scientific name for Emily's Mouse. Soon scientists all over the world will know about Emily's Mouse."

"It's soooo cute," Emily said, patting its tiny head. "What will you do with it?"

"We'll do what we always do. We'll take its picture and then let it go," Malcolm Mousefinder explained. "Hey, Dad, look!

She's got an eye on the end of her finger!"

"All the better to rescue you with," Emily said, pointing it at him.

Everyone laughed except Malcolm, who looked puzzled.

And that's how a very rare mouse came to be named after Emily.

10

Emily Eyefinger,
Crook Catcher

One day Emily was in a bank with her mother when two masked men and a masked woman burst in. They had guns and pointed them in every direction.

"Get down on the floor!" the woman screamed. "We're the Bad Luck Gang and this is a holdup!"

"What's a holdup?" Emily asked.

"Shhh," her mother said. "We'd better do as they say, dear."

All the customers had to lie facedown on

the floor with their eyes closed and their hands on their heads. Of course with her hands on top of her head, Emily could see everything with her eyefinger. She watched as the robbers took all the money and stuffed it into suitcases.

"Now I know what a holdup is," Emily said to her mother. "It's like robbing, isn't it?"

"Quiet!" one of the robbers ordered. "No talking while we're robbing!"

When the robbers were about to leave the bank, they told everyone to lie still and count to six hundred with their eyes closed. Then they walked out, taking off their masks and whistling a tune so no one on the street would think they were bank robbers. No one outside even noticed them.

". . . eleven, twelve, thirteen . . .," the people in the bank said all together.

"You can stop counting," Emily said when the robbers had driven away. "They've gone."

"How do you know?" someone whispered.

"I peeked," Emily said, wiggling her eye-finger.

"My goodness," everyone said at once. "That little girl has an eye on the end of her finger."

"It's very handy," Emily said.

When the police heard that it was the Bad Luck Gang, they looked glum.

"Those people are too smart for us," the sergeant said. "I don't think we'll ever be able to catch the Bad Luck Gang. No one knows what they look like because they always wear masks."

"I know what they look like," Emily said. "I saw their faces."

"You what?" the sergeant said.

"I said, 'I saw their faces.'"

"But they had masks on."

"They took them off just before they left the bank," Emily explained.

"But you said you were lying facedown

on the floor. How could you possibly have seen them?"

Emily showed them her eyefinger.

"With this," she said.

The sergeant looked surprised, just as Emily thought she would.

"Why, you've got an eye right on the end of your finger," she said.

"I've had it all my life," Emily said proudly.

The other police officers gathered around her.

"How can we get one?" one of them asked.

"They don't grow on trees, you know," Emily said.

"No, I'm sure they don't."

"If you weren't born with one," Emily explained, "I'm afraid you'll never have one. I'm sorry but that's just the way it is."

In a minute the police sergeant had Emily looking through a stack of photographs of bank robbing suspects. And in two minutes

Emily had found pictures of the three people who called themselves the Bad Luck Gang.

"She was one of them and the other two are here and here," she said, pointing to the photographs.

"Right!" the sergeant said. "Let's go and get them."

And in a little more than three minutes the robbers were caught and put in jail.

"That little girl actually has an eye on the end of her finger," the woman bank robber said later to the two men bank robbers. "That was bad luck for us. I guess we really are the Bad Luck Gang."

"You mean we *were* the Bad Luck Gang," one of the men bank robbers said with a tear in his eye. "We're not even a gang anymore. We're just three bad luck prisoners."

The police were so pleased with Emily that they gave her a special medal. They asked if they could call her when they needed help.

"Of course you may," Emily said, rubbing the medal to make it shiny. "I'm always happy to help."

And so Emily grew and grew. She got used to being different, although it wasn't easy. Having an eye on the end of her finger did have its problems.

Every now and then her parents would ask, "Do you still like having that eye on your finger?"

Emily would smile and hold up both hands.

"On the one hand, I like it," Emily said, looking at the hand with her eyefinger. Then she'd turn to the other hand and say, "But on the other hand, I don't."

This was Emily's little joke and the Eyefingers all laughed. And when they finished laughing, they laughed some more.

About the author

Although he was born in Boston, Duncan Ball has spent much of his life abroad, in Anchorage, Madrid, Paris, and now Sydney, where he lives with his wife, Jill, a violist.

Duncan Ball has written many books for children that were published in Australia, and recently he has begun to be published in his native land. *Emily Eyefinger* is his only book to be published first for American readers.

About the illustrator

George Ulrich lives in Marblehead, Massachusetts. He was graduated from Syracuse University with a degree in fine arts and has illustrated many popular books for young readers, including the titles in the Creepy Creature Club series by Stephen Mooser and *The Million Dollar Potato* by Louis Phillips.